HIDDEN IN THE OVERWORLD

W9-BXS-266

HIDDEN IN THE OVERWORLD

AN UNOFFICIAL LEAGUE OF GRIEFERS ADVENTURE, #2

Winter Morgan

Sky Pony Press
New York

This book is not authorized or sponsored by Mojang AB, Notch Development AB or Scholastic Inc., or any other person or entity owning or controlling rights in the Minecraft name, trademark, or copyrights.

Copyright © 2015 by Hollan Publishing, Inc.

First box set edition 2016.

Minecraft® is a registered trademark of Notch Development AB

The Minecraft game is copyright © Mojang AB

All rights reserved. No part of this book may be reproduced in any manner without the express written consent of the publisher, except in the case of brief excerpts in critical reviews or articles. All inquiries should be addressed to Sky Pony Press, 307 West 36th Street, 11th Floor, New York, NY 10018.

Sky Pony Press books may be purchased in bulk at special discounts for sales promotion, corporate gifts, fund-raising, or educational purposes. Special editions can also be created to specifications. For details, contact the Special Sales Department, Sky Pony Press, 307 West 36th Street, 11th Floor, New York, NY 10018 or info@skyhorsepublishing.com.

Sky Pony® is a registered trademark of Skyhorse Publishing, Inc.®, a Delaware corporation.

Minecraft® is a registered trademark of Notch Development AB.
The Minecraft game is copyright © Mojang AB.

Visit our website at www.skyponypress.com.

10 9 8 7 6 5 4 3 2

Library of Congress Cataloging-in-Publication Data is available on file.

Cover design by Brian Peterson
Cover photo by Megan Miller

Box set ISBN: 978-1-5107-0477-0
Ebook ISBN: 978-1-63450-596-3

Printed in China

TABLE OF CONTENTS

HIDDEN IN THE OVERWORLD

1
REBUILDING

"**W**ow, this tree is hard to chop down," Noah gasped as he swung his axe into a large tree. He was helping Violet gather supplies to aid in the rebuilding of the town.

"We need as much wood as we can chop. I want to build the most elaborate tree house in the Overworld," Violet said while she collected wood from the tree and began crafting.

The sun was shining brightly as Violet made her way up the tree and put down the wooden planks. Since the town was freed of Daniel and his army of griefers, there was a flurry of rebuilding and rejoicing. The village shops were open for trading and everyone was free to pursue their own activities in the Overworld. Explorers set out exploring, farmers grew crops, and alchemists made potions. The Overworld was back to normal. The only enemies the townspeople had to fight now were hostile mobs that struck at night. There was an air of happiness in the town. Everyone smiled, relieved that they could live as they pleased.

Violet placed more wooden planks in the tree high above the town. She looked out at the water.

"Once we're done building, we should go underneath the water and see if there's an ocean monument with treasure," Violet said, and Noah agreed.

Hannah, Violet's friend who was an expert alchemist, climbed up the ladder toward Violet.

"Violet," Hannah called. "Do you need any help?"

"Will you grab some wooden planks?" Violet asked. She placed a wide plank, creating a base for the house. "I was also wondering if you'd like to explore the Ocean Biome with me when I'm done building. I bet you have a potion of Water Breathing."

"That sounds like fun," Hannah replied with enthusiasm as she handed another wooden plank to Violet.

"It's so nice to live in such a calm world. I was exhausted from living in terror when Daniel and his army were in the town." Violet smiled, but as she stood on the wooden planks, her smile disappeared. The sky grew dark, and it began to rain. Violet was suspicious. "That's odd. It's raining," Violet said as she climbed down to the ground.

"Zombies!" Noah shouted.

A cluster of zombies advanced into the center of the village. Noah dashed toward the village with his enchanted diamond sword.

"Why is this happening?" Hannah questioned.

"There's no time to wonder why—we have to help Noah!" Violet replied, and the two hurried toward their friend.

Although there was no time to question why the attack was happening, Violet had to admit that she felt there was something more sinister at play than a naturally generated zombie attack. The sudden rain and the zombie attack came the day after the town's iron golem was destroyed. The town still hadn't figured out who had demolished the golem. And without any protection from the golem, they were being attacked by the menacing creatures of the night.

The zombies tore the doors off the village library and the butcher shop. Violet struck a zombie with a sword, but it had already attacked a villager, transforming it into a zombie villager.

"Help!" Valentino the Butcher called out.

The trio bolted into the shop, sneaking up behind the zombie and clobbering the vacant-eyed beast with their swords.

"Oh no!" Valentino cried out, and his eyes widened when five zombies lumbered into his shop.

Noah, Violet, and Hannah found themselves cornered inside Valentino's small butcher shop as the zombies outnumbered them. Violet lunged at one zombie, striking it, but it still attacked her. She was weakened. Hannah struggled to defeat two zombies while Noah attacked the remaining zombies. Even as Noah defeated the zombies, a new batch entered the butcher shop.

"This is neverending," Violet said in exhaustion. Her health bar was dangerously low.

Ben and Angela raced through the door and joined the battle. They were full of energy and obliterated the rest of the zombies.

The rain was still falling while in the distance more zombies spawned and followed the grassy path into the heart of the village. The group tried to stop the invasion, but zombies attacked the villagers, and, one by one, shopkeepers, librarians, and a preacher were transformed into zombie villagers, making the battle even more challenging. Hannah splashed potions on the zombie villagers in an attempt to save them and turn them back into peaceful villagers.

An army of zombies marched through the town.

A townsperson wearing diamond armor and toting a powerful enchanted sword shouted at Violet, "If you didn't run Daniel out of this town, he'd protect us from this invasion. We never had attacks from hostile mobs when Daniel was in charge."

Violet was shocked by this comment. She knew she had saved the town from Daniel, and didn't realize any inhabitants actually liked having Daniel around. Were there townspeople who actually sided with the evil Daniel?

As Violet battled more zombies, the sun came out. The bright solar rays destroyed the zombies.

"We're safe!" Noah exclaimed.

"Not really," Ben said in a shaky voice. "Look!"

An Ender Dragon swept through the sky.

"See!" The diamond-armored townsperson called out. "This is awful. You ruined our town."

"Ruined the town? I saved our village from a tyrannical leader," Violet asserted defensively.

"Take this," Hannah said as she handed a potion of Strength to Violet. Then Hannah stood in front of the townsperson and shouted, "Violet saved this town. I'd rather battle mobs and get to live the life I want than live under the laws of a cruel leader."

"But the Ender Dragon is flying over our town. Our lives are ruined and our town will be destroyed," the harassing townsperson called out.

"I'll bet your friend Daniel is behind this attack," Violet replied and swiftly shot an arrow at the beast that flew through the sunny sky.

"He's not my friend. I just liked being protected," said the townsperson, who also took out his bow and arrow and shot at the Ender Dragon.

"This isn't going to be an easy battle, but we'll win it together. And Daniel wasn't protecting you, he was controlling you," Violet stated while she shot more arrows, striking the powerful black dragon with purple eyes.

The Ender Dragon's purple health bar remained strong. The gang shot arrows, but its health didn't diminish.

"Once we defeat this dragon, we have to find out who summoned it," Noah exclaimed as he shot an arrow.

"I think you mean, *if* we defeat the Ender Dragon. This dragon seems to have a super-powerful energy supply," cautioned Violet. She wasn't sure they'd win this battle, until she saw a slew of townspeople emerge from their homes, dressed in armor. In unison, they unleashed a deluge of arrows at the scaly dragon.

The dragon swooped down striking the group. The townspeople huddled together to avoid the attack, but it didn't save them.

"This is all your fault!" the townsperson wearing diamond armor called out.

Violet struck the beast with an arrow. Ben threw snowballs. A fisherman ran toward the dragon, hitting it with a fishing rod. Yet the dragon still had enough energy to lunge at the group. It was an endless battle.

"We can do it!" Violet said breathlessly, but even as these words fell from her mouth, she wasn't sure she believed them.

2
IT'S NOT THE END

The dragon's piercing purple eyes glared at Violet as the beast rushed at her.

"Help!" Violet called out, fumbling with her arrow.

Noah stepped in front of the dragon, and with perfect aim, he struck the creature. The fierce beast lit up as it exploded across the bright sky. A lone dragon egg dropped on the ground. Hannah pointed at the portal to the End, which had surfaced in their village.

"Look!" Hannah walked toward the portal and said, "Let's go."

Violet stared at the portal, stuttering, "I d-d-don't want to go to the End."

"We can get a lot of good resources," remarked Hannah, "and there's another dragon we must slay."

Hannah stood on the portal.

"We can't let her go alone!" Ben called out as he hurried to join Hannah. Noah and Violet followed. Within seconds, they emerged into the dark world of the

End. The group crowded together on a small obsidian platform.

A roar was heard in the distance. Two Endermen approached the gang.

"Don't look at them!" Violet told the others.

A shriek rent the air. One of the Endermen teleported next to Hannah, and she threw a potion of Weakening on the Enderman, while Noah struck it with his diamond sword.

Roar!

They could hear the Ender Dragon's wings flapping as the beast flew high above in the dark sky, past an obsidian pillar, only stopping to ingest Ender crystals.

Noah shot an arrow at the Ender crystals.

Kaboom!

The crystals exploded, but the dragon wasn't harmed. It lunged at the group, letting out another roar.

"I have snowballs," said Ben as he threw one at the creature, but the Ender crystals had given the dragon incredible strength and power.

The dragon struck Ben with its wing. Ben flew through the air and into the darkness.

"Ben!" screamed Hannah.

"He's gone," Noah said in shock, "but we have to beat this dragon!"

Hannah shot another arrow, piercing the dragon's dark flesh. The dragon flew toward Hannah, but Noah shielded her with his diamond sword.

"I hit Ender crystals!" Violet shouted gleefully as the crystals exploded. The dragon's energy was diminishing.

"We have to destroy the rest of the crystals; it's our only chance."

Noah struck the dragon again. It wailed in pain and struggled to reach the Ender crystals. Violet aimed at the remaining Ender crystals. The dragon was only inches from the crystals when Violet shot her arrow and the crystals exploded. Hannah shot an arrow at the weakened dragon.

"Bull's-eye!" exclaimed Noah when he struck the last batch of Ender crystals. Hannah and Violet flooded the dragon with a sea of arrows, depleting its health bar.

"I think we got this one!" But Noah was too confident.

"Look!" Hannah shouted. "Over there!"

A group of Endermen walked toward them.

"We can't battle both!" Hannah was worried.

"We have to try," Noah exclaimed as he shot two more arrows at the dragon, which flew toward him.

Violet lunged at the dragon with a diamond sword, but the flying beast tossed Violet from the obsidian ground, and she was lost into the oblivion.

Noah used all of his might to strike the dragon, while Hannah struggled to fight the Endermen. One Enderman shrieked and hit Hannah. She pounded the Enderman with her sword, but its energy level was high, and hers was low.

Two more Endermen shrieked and teleported next to Hannah. She was surrounded. Hannah fumbled for her potions, but an Enderman attacked her, and Hannah was destroyed.

Noah was alone in the End. He shot an arrow at the dragon as the Endermen crept toward him. He feared it was a losing battle, but shot one last arrow at the dragon. He was shocked when the dragon began to explode and dropped an egg. He raced toward the portal back to the Overworld.

Noah hopped on the portal. Within seconds he found himself alone in a sandy biome.

"Hello!" A voice called out from the distance.

3
SEARCHING

The sun was setting in the desert biome. Noah looked for the person who called to him. "Who's there?" he asked.

"Can't you see me?" The mysterious voice carried through the dim evening sky.

"No, where are you?" Noah asked, as he quickly scanned the area searching for shelter.

"I'm on the steps of a desert temple. Come here. It's safe."

Noah didn't trust this unseen person. It could be one of Daniel's griefers. He was sure they were hiding somewhere in the Overworld. Noah eyed the area for a desert temple. When he spotted the temple he cautiously walked toward it and saw a man with green hair, suited up in diamond armor, standing in front of the majestic sandstone temple.

"Come quickly," the stranger called out.

As the night sky set in, Noah sprinted to the desert temple. "Who are you?"

This stranger with the green hair led Noah past the center of the temple. Noah kept a close look at the ground as he followed him farther into the temple. He searched for the blue clay block to signify there was treasure in the temple. He was running low on resources and hoped he'd find a chest filled with gold ingots or another treasure.

"If you're looking for treasure, the temple was emptied," said the stranger as they walked down the hall to a small room with a bed. "You can stay here for the night. I've fortified the temple with lots of torches, so you'll be safe."

"Why are you being so nice to me?" asked Noah.

"If I see someone who is in need, I like to help them."

"Who are you?" Noah repeated his question, but he didn't get a response.

"It's late. You need to sleep," the green-haired person replied and left.

Noah was sleepy as he pulled the wool covers over his body. When he awoke, he searched the temple for the green-haired stranger, but he was nowhere to be found. Noah walked out of the temple onto the sandy ground.

"Hi," the green-haired man appeared and offered Noah an apple.

Noah took a bite and asked, "Are you going to tell me who you are?"

"My name is Harrison," he said as he too chomped on an apple. "I'm an explorer."

"Are you the one who emptied the treasure?"

"No, it was gone when I got here."

"How long have you been here?" asked Noah.

"I'm not sure, it's been a long time though. I can't go back to my village; it was taken over by a man named Daniel and his rainbow griefer army."

"Harrison, where are you from?" Noah questioned. He couldn't believe the rainbow griefers had already taken over another village.

Harrison looked off into the distance when he replied, "I lived in a village located by the Ocean Biome."

Noah had a sudden thought about Harrison's town. "I think you might be from my town."

"Your town? You don't look familiar." Harrison was suspicious.

"My town was also taken over by rainbow griefers, but we fought them off," Noah said proudly of their victory.

"Really? I wish that had happened to my town. I'd love to go home," Harrison said wistfully.

Noah took another bite of his apple and began to think. "Was there a butcher named Valentino in your town?" he asked.

"Yes, there was!" exclaimed Harrison.

"We're from the same town." Noah was excited and spoke quickly, "I can take you back with me. You can be reunited with your friends."

"Really? The griefers are gone?" Harrison was overjoyed.

"They were gone when I left, but somebody summoned the Ender Dragon and our town had to come together to battle the evil beast." Noah wondered if Daniel and his awful army had returned when he was fighting in the End.

The two made their way past the Desert Biome and through a grassy area. A cow was grazing peacefully.

"Should we hunt it?" asked Harrison.

"No, we have enough food in our inventory. But we might want to keep moving; we have to trek through the snowy mountainous Taiga Biome, and I want to do that before dark." Noah was worried that they'd reach the top of the mountain in the dark, and they'd be vulnerable to other attacks.

Yet when they reached the snowy biome Noah took time to stop and pick up snow. "You should take some snow and craft snowballs; they are very handy to have."

Noah crafted a bunch of snowballs and placed them in his inventory. Harrison stared at the enormous mountain that stood in front of them. "Do we have to climb that mountain to make our way back to the village?"

"Yes. It's a challenge, but we can do it." Noah climbed up the snowy mountain as Harrison followed.

They stopped at the top of the mountain and looked out at the horizon. "I can see our village," Noah said when he spotted the new iron golem that looked over their peaceful village.

"We're almost there!" Harrison called out.

"It's farther than it appears," warned Noah, "and we'd better start moving along because it will be dark soon."

They made their way down the mountain, and suddenly stumbled across a cave.

"Should we stop here and mine?" asked Harrison.

"Maybe we can place torches around the cave, so we can stay there for the night. I don't want to get stuck in the dark." Noah inspected the cave, walking slowly into the murky interior.

Harrison placed a torch by the entrance. He heard Noah call out, "Help!"

A horde of cave spiders surrounded him. Noah struck them with his enchanted diamond sword, but he wasn't able to destroy all of the spiders.

"I think I've been bitten!" Noah shouted.

Harrison rushed to Noah's side, striking spiders and handing Noah a vial of milk. "Drink this."

The two battled the spiders. Noah called out, "I see a spawner in the corner." He rushed toward it, using all of the torches in his inventory to destroy the cave spider spawner.

Harrison struck a cluster of spiders. Only a few remained and Noah helped Harrison destroy them.

Noah took out his pickaxe and dug deep within the ground. "Since we're here, we should see if there are any diamonds."

They dug with their pickaxes until Noah called out, "Diamonds!" A layer of blue surfaced, and they eagerly unearthed the gems.

As they were about to place them in their inventory a voice called out, "Hand over those diamonds now!"

4
SURVIVAL IN THE SWAMP

Noah aimed his powerful enchanted sword at a stranger dressed in diamond armor and sunglasses.

The newcomer charged toward Noah with his sword out. Harrison and Noah both struck the aggressor, depleting his energy.

"Stop!" pleaded the person wearing sunglasses. "Okay, you can keep the diamonds."

Noah held his sword close to the man. "Why shouldn't we destroy you?"

"You tried to steal our diamonds!" shouted Harrison.

"I'm desperate," begged the outsider. "I have nothing. My energy is so low, I'm only a strike away from being destroyed. If I respawn, I'll wake up in a terrible place and I never want to go back there."

"Where are you from?" Noah questioned.

"I was a prisoner."

"Who did that to you?" Harrison asked.

"I'm not sure who he was, but he wasn't alone. He had two rainbow griefers with him."

Noah's heart skipped a beat as he questioned, "Did you say rainbow griefers?"

"Yes."

"Where did they keep you?" asked Harrison.

The stranger in the sunglasses told them his story. "I was exploring an ocean monument when I came up to the surface of the water for air. My potion of Underwater Breathing was running low. As I swam toward the beach, a man approached me. He was with two rainbow griefers. He demanded that I hand over any treasures I had in my inventory. I tried to fight them, but they overpowered me. At first I thought they would destroy me and get my stuff and I'd respawn in a cabin I had built, but the man said I looked useful. They captured me and put me in a bedrock room. I couldn't escape."

"Where was the bedrock room?" asked Noah.

"How did you escape?" questioned Harrison.

There were many questions circulating in their minds, and they were overwhelming the tired stranger in sunglasses. "Please. One at a time. I promise to answer all of your questions.

"The bedrock room was inside a cave in the Jungle Biome. I escaped because my captors moved to a new location and they just left me there. I spent days in the room without food. Once I realized they were gone, I felt brave enough to try and escape. I dug a hole in the dirt ceiling. And then I found you guys."

"That's awful. I'm glad you escaped," said Noah.

"What's your name?" asked Harrison.

"I'm Elias."

"Elias, we are Harrison and Noah, and you're welcome to head back with us. We have to get home. We believe the same people are also attacking our village. They summoned the Ender Dragon to attack our townspeople in the middle of the day," explained Noah.

Elias followed Noah and Harrison toward their town. They reached the Swamp Biome as evening was setting in, and the sky was getting dark. Noah looked up and said, "We have to build some shelter."

A bat flew close to Noah's head. Harrison cried out, "Look—a witch hut!"

A witch hut with potted mushrooms on the window-sill had spawned right in front of them. A witch emerged from the hut and scuffled toward the trio, clutching a potion in her hand. The group took out their swords and bows and arrows, but the witch splashed them with a potion of Weakness, lowering their health bars and slowing them down.

Noah tried to shoot an arrow at the witch, but he was too weak. Harrison grabbed some milk from his inventory and took a sip. He regained his energy and rushed toward her with his diamond sword, striking the purple-robed witch.

Noah also drank some milk and then handed the bottle to Elias. When the milk had worked its magic, they joined Harrison in the battle. The witch drank a potion of Healing, but she was outnumbered and defeated. Six pieces of glowstone dropped on the ground, so they quickly picked it up and placed it in their inventories.

The group began to craft a crude cabin to spend the night in when they heard a bouncing sound. "Slimes!" Harrison pointed at two green blocks hopping toward them.

Noah put down the wooden planks he was using to build the cabin and struck a green slime with his sword.

The slimes broke into smaller cubes. Noah, Harrison, and Elias struggled to fight the array of cubes that jumped at them.

Noah clobbered a larger slime as Harrison warned, "Don't fall in the water."

Noah was so immersed in obliterating the slimes, he didn't notice that he stood on the edge of a body of murky swamp water. A group of bats flew past as Noah struck a large slime with his sword. Harrison and Elias helped Noah battle the smaller slimes.

"It looks like we defeated all the slimes," Noah said in relief as he looked out in the distance.

"We need to build this cabin fast. I have to sleep here. If not, I'll respawn in that bedrock jail, and the rainbow griefers could be back there," said Elias.

Noah tried to craft the cabin as quickly as he could. He wished Violet were with him. He was rather lazy with his building skills since she was a master builder and was able to craft makeshift homes in a matter of minutes, while he was still trying to make a door for the house.

Harrison and Elias helped him, but they could hear more slimes bouncing in their direction.

"We'll take care of those slimy beasts. You just keep building the house," Elias told Noah.

Noah worked as fast as he could. He was almost done with the external structure and then had to craft beds for the gang.

Harrison and Elias used nearly all of their last bits of energy to defeat the slimes. Both of them were struck by the slimes and their health bars were dangerously low. Just in time, Noah finished the house and destroyed the remaining slimes.

"We need to get to bed," Noah said.

The trio hurried inside the house, crawled underneath blue wool blankets, and fell asleep. They didn't get to sleep very long though, because within minutes the sun had risen. It was a new day. And there was a suspicious noise coming from outside their door.

"What's that?" Harrison's voice wavered as he asked that question.

"I'm not sure." Noah walked to the small window to investigate the banging sound that boomed in the distance.

Kaboom!

"It looks like there was an explosion!" exclaimed Noah. He could see smoke, but wasn't sure what had been destroyed.

Noah could see a rainbow griefer sprint past a patch of giant mushrooms.

5
BACK HOME

"**A**re you sure it was a rainbow griefer?" asked Harrison.

"Do you think maybe they're following me?" worried Elias.

"We need to head back to our village. We have to warn Violet," Noah said as they set out toward the village, and into the Jungle Biome thick with leaves.

"I can't see," Elias remarked as he took out shears and cleared a path.

"The village isn't far from here." Noah led the way.

"It's been so long since I've been home," Harrison said as he brushed his green hair from his face. He had forgotten a lot about the village, but when they approached the town and Harrison spotted the village streets, everything became familiar to him.

The trio walked down the busy village streets, past the library and the locksmith's shop.

"There's Valentino the Butcher!" Harrison called out and hurried over to his old friend.

"Harrison!" Valentino was stunned to see him. "It's been ages. How did you find your way back?"

"I have to thank my new friend Noah."

Noah walked over with Elias and introduced him to Valentino.

"Noah, you are a good person," remarked Valentino the Butcher. "You saved me from the zombies and you've reunited me with an old dear friend, Harrison, and also introduced me to a new friend, Elias."

Violet spotted Noah in town and rushed toward him. "You're back!" She was extremely excited to see him.

"Have there been any more attacks from the Ender Dragon?" Noah asked as he looked nervously up at the sunny sky.

"No, things have been calm here. So, you must have defeated the Ender Dragon in the End?" Violet was impressed.

"Yes, it wasn't easy. I spawned in the desert and met Harrison. And then we met Elias." He introduced them to Violet.

Violet wanted to show Noah the tree house. Since he was gone she had made serious progress on it. One portion of the lavish, scenic building was completed. Noah and his new friends followed Violet to the tree house. He told Violet the story of Daniel and the rainbow griefers capturing Elias. Noah finished by stating, "I'm pretty sure I saw a rainbow griefer in the swamp outside of the village. They had blown something up with TNT."

"Did you see what they blew up?" questioned Violet, as she climbed the ladder up to the tree house.

"No, I wanted to make my way back here. We were running low on resources and I also wanted your help."

Harrison told Violet how difficult it was to build a house quickly. "Noah told us you are one of the best builders in the Overworld," Harrison said as he looked around the grand tree house. "I guess he wasn't exaggerating."

"Thanks. But there is no time to tour the tree house now; we have to find Daniel and the rainbow griefers before they attack us or other innocent people. I can't relax knowing that they are so close to us." Violet walked into her tree house bedroom and opened a chest containing her armor and swords. She filled her inventory with all the resources she needed to battle the griefers. "Does anybody need anything?"

The trio looked through their inventories and used Violet's crafting table and anvil to create powerful swords and armor.

"We need Hannah to brew potions with this glowstone," Noah said to Violet.

"Yes, she should come with us on our journey to find these evil rainbow griefers. We can't just wait here until they attack us. We have to go find them." Violet had suited up in armor. She climbed down the ladder and walked to Hannah's house.

Hannah and Ben were farming. Ben was happy to see Noah had returned to the village.

"You beat the Ender Dragon!" Hannah exclaimed.

"Yes, but I also found rainbow griefers in the swamp and we have to battle them," replied Noah.

Hannah and Ben filled their inventories with supplies. Everybody was ready to hunt for rainbow griefers.

"The sun is setting," Violet said as she looked at the darkened sky. "I think we should wait until morning."

They all agreed to meet in front of Hannah's house at daybreak. Noah and the others walked back to the tree house for the night.

"I hate losing time. I wish we could just leave now." Violet was upset.

"Try to be patient. If we left now, it would be a losing battle," reasoned Noah.

Harrison and Elias were excited to spend the night in a tree house. They quickened their pace as they neared the house and the sky grew darker. When they approached the ladder, a spider jockey jumped out from behind the tree trunk and shot an arrow at Violet. She was still wearing her armor, so it didn't affect her.

Noah shot an arrow at the spider jockey, but it lunged at the group and avoided his arrow. Harrison's arrow hit the spider, weakening the evil arachnoid. Violet shot arrows at the skeleton.

"I got it!" Elias delivered the final blow to the skeleton while the others rushed to destroy the spider. Harrison swung his diamond sword at the mob, obliterating it.

The skeleton dropped an arrow and the spider dropped a spider's eye.

"We should get some sleep," Violet said as she climbed the ladder. She stopped abruptly when she saw a group of skeletons advancing through the village streets.

6
ON THE ROAD AGAIN

An arrow streaked across the night sky, hitting Noah. As skeletons filled the village streets, the townspeople emerged from their homes to defend themselves from the invasion. Arrows flew everywhere, and the skeletons were slowly being destroyed by the townspeople who attacked the bony menaces.

"Get him!" Elias shouted to Noah, warning him about a skeleton sneaking up from behind.

Noah struck the skeleton with his sword, as more skeletons filled the village streets. Noah was suspicious of the attack. He wondered if Daniel and the rainbow griefers were spawning skeletons outside of the town. He fought hard all through the night. The gang needed to find Daniel and the rainbow griefers and stop them from attacking their town.

The last skeleton was finally destroyed and dropped a bow. Noah picked it up and placed it in his inventory. There was still a while before morning would arrive.

Violet suggested they rest. "Let's all sleep in the tree house so if we get destroyed, we'll respawn here."

Harrison, Hannah, Ben, Noah, and Elias followed Violet up the tree house ladder. Violet showed them a large room filled with beds. "This is my guest room. We should all stay in here for the night."

Everyone climbed into a bed and got underneath the wool covers. It was hard to sleep. They were eager to start their journey to find Daniel and the rainbow griefers that were hidden in the Overworld.

Soon the sun shined through the large picture window of the tree house. Violet got up and offered, "Let's go into my kitchen, where I have some cake."

"Cake!" Elias was thrilled.

The group stood in the rustic kitchen with views of the village. As they ate the cake, they looked out the window and saw the village coming to life in the early morning sun. The shops were opening. The village librarian walked through the town. They could see Valentino the Butcher heading for his shop.

"I'm going to miss this town when I'm away," Hannah commented and took a bite of her cake.

"If we don't go on this mission, we can't save it," Violet admonished her. "We'll return, and Daniel and his evil griefers will realize that they can't attack this town anymore. We aren't afraid of them and they can't terrorize us."

"I can't live here if they take over this town again; that was just awful," Ben remarked as he suited up in armor and double-checked his inventory.

"I have an inventory full of potions," announced Hannah. "I think we'll be fine."

"I wouldn't use the word *fine*," added Violet. "This isn't going to be an easy battle, but we will get through it."

With stomachs comfortably full of cake, the group strolled down the village streets and headed toward the lush green biome outside of town. A wild ocelot dashed past them, but they avoided the creature. Ben had to leave his dog Hope behind, and they all agreed not to take in any more pets. This was going to be a difficult journey and they needed to concentrate on finding the griefers. There was no time for any distractions.

When the group reached the jungle biome, they heard a noise in the distance. They hid behind a thick patch of leaves and stood still.

"It sounds like voices," whispered Hannah.

"I see a purple leg," Violet said as she poked her head through the leaves.

"Griefers!" Noah was ready to pounce.

"Stop," warned Violet. "We need to follow them and see where they're going. We don't want them to see us. Trust me, it will be better if we stage a grand scale surprise attack."

The others agreed. They attempted to shelter themselves with as many leaves as they could find, then stood silently and waited for the two purple griefers to walk past.

Violet held her breath. Noah's heart beat fast. And the purple griefers soon passed by.

When the griefers were still visible but out of earshot Violet said to the others, "Let's go." The group trailed cautiously behind the purple griefers.

The griefers walked on a cleared path and went into a large house.

"I wonder who built that house—it's very nice," Violet declared as she studied the wooden structure built on four stilts that made it rise above the verdant jungle. On either side of the house were two flaming torches. The one side of the house had a porch where two orange griefers stood looking out.

"We must make sure nobody sees us," Noah told them. "We have to find out if Daniel is hiding in this house."

The purple griefers entered the home. As the group studied the area around the house, they observed a large body of water behind the house. It wasn't deep enough to house an ocean monument, but they could take shelter in the water if they drank a potion of Underwater Breathing.

"We can't just storm into this house," said Ben. "We have to come up with a good plan."

"I've eyed the area for various escape plans," Violet announced, and she listed the many places they could hide from the griefers, including the water behind the wooden house.

"Look!" Noah tried to keep his voice down, but he was nervous and it was hard to regulate the sound.

The group watched Daniel and a band of six red griefers walk out of the house. They stood silently as Daniel and the rainbow griefers passed just inches from the group. Everyone was worried they'd be captured. When Daniel and the griefers walked deep into the jungle, the gang collectively let out a sigh of relief. They were safe for that moment.

"We should try and enter the house now while Daniel is gone," suggested Violet, and she started toward it.

"What about making a plan?" asked Noah.

"Nevermind that. Follow me!" instructed Violet as she walked confidently toward the wooden house. "And get your diamond swords out."

Violet walked underneath the four stilts that held the house up. On one side of the house she saw a small staircase leading to the entrance. The others followed Violet as she climbed the stairs.

The only thing that could be heard was the sound of their hearts. They beat fast as Violet opened the door.

"We're under attack!" a griefer called out from inside the house.

Noah rushed at a green griefer with his diamond sword, but an arrow struck him.

"Help!" Ben called out.

As the group each dealt with an intense battle of their own, they caught a glimpse of Ben surrounded by a horde of orange griefers.

7

CREATURES OF THE NIGHT

"Tell me where Daniel was going!" shouted Violet as she cornered a purple griefer, pointing her diamond sword at the griefer's rainbow-colored head.

"Never!" the griefer retorted.

"What is he planning?" she demanded.

"I'll never tell you!"

Violet struck the griefer and he was destroyed. She helped Ben battle the griefers that were quickly damaging his energy level. Ben was about to be weakened. Hannah gave him some milk, but she was struck as she handed it to him. Noah took a block of TNT out of his inventory and yelled to his friends, "Get out of here now!"

The gang dashed toward the exit. Noah followed, carrying the block of TNT, and ignited it by the entrance.

Kaboom!

The majestic jungle home was destroyed, along with the evil griefers who were living there.

"Daniel isn't going to be happy about this," Noah said as he looked at the charred remains of the house.

"Like we care," Hannah joked to Noah.

"You did a good job," Violet said with a smile.

"Now we have to find Daniel," said Noah, and he looked off in the direction they had seen Daniel travel. "He went this way," Noah said as he trekked farther into the jungle, hoping they were going in the right direction.

"It's going to be night soon," Harrison remarked. "We should build some shelter."

"No problem. I can do it." Violet began to gather all the supplies for building, and she crafted a house large enough for all of them.

The group gathered inside and helped Violet craft beds. The gang was about to climb into their beds when they heard a noise outside.

"We have to see if it's the rainbow griefers," Violet said, and she went to the window. A purple griefer walked near the house, but a creeper was silently lurking behind the lone griefer.

Kaboom! The creeper destroyed the purple griefer.

"We aren't safe here," Ben stammered.

"We need to sleep. It would be worse if we were outside," replied Hannah.

The group covered themselves with wool blankets and drifted into a peaceful slumber until they were awakened by a blast.

Violet rushed to the window and saw smoke rising in the distance. "I don't know where the smoke is coming from, but there are a group of zombies heading toward us."

As the words left Violet's mouth, a zombie ripped the door off the hinges of their hastily constructed home.

"Not my best work," Violet joked about the door. She suited up and grabbed her sword, hitting the vacant-eyed creature of the night in the chest.

Harrison shot arrows at the zombies breaking into the small house.

"Gotcha!" shouted Elias as he struck a zombie with his sword.

The group dashed from the house, only to find themselves surrounded by zombies.

One zombie lumbered toward Noah with its arms extended. The black-eyed brute lashed out at Noah, and he struck the beast with his diamond sword.

"I've never seen this many zombies before," Hannah said in disbelief, when a large group of zombies emerged from behind a jungle tree.

It was dark and the zombies' purple pants stood out in the dim atmosphere. Since they were in the thick of the jungle, the battle was even more intense. Patches of leaves obscured some of the zombies. As soon as the gang finished battling one bunch of zombies, another group would jump out from behind the leaves.

Hannah threw a potion of Healing on two zombies that were hidden behind the bark of a large tree and destroyed the creatures. Elias struck zombies with his diamond sword. Harrison shot more arrows at the zombies. Yet no matter how many zombies they killed, more appeared on the horizon.

"I bet the rainbow griefers are behind this zombie attack," Violet said. She struck a zombie with her sword, while another zombie hit her back.

"We're losing energy!" Noah cried out as two zombies struck him. He was extremely weak and used all of his remaining energy to fight the zombie that stood inches from him.

Violet ran to Noah's side and slammed the zombie with her sword.

"Help us!" Ben called out in desperation. Hannah and Ben were trapped in the middle of a circle of zombies, so Violet and Noah rushed to help them defeat the evil dead beasts.

Elias was cornered by the edge of the water. He used his sword to strike the zombies but they outnumbered him. Harrison rushed over to back up his friend, but they were both dangerously close to the edge. They didn't want to fall into the deep blue water in the middle of the night.

Ben, Hannah, Violet, and Noah hurried toward them and used all of their might to defeat the zombies that were attacking their friends.

"I don't think we can keep this up," Noah said wearily as he destroyed yet another zombie.

"I agree!" Violet struck a zombie and realized that she was both hungry and tired. If she didn't get something to eat soon, she would respawn in the tree house and would have to start the mission all over again.

Ben clobbered a zombie and stated, "That might be the last one I can fight." He was also running low on energy.

Luckily, just when the group's health bars were almost diminished, the sun began to rise.

Hannah passed around potions of Healing to her friends. Their energy bars began refueling.

"We're saved!" Hannah shouted in relief.

"Let's hold off on any celebrations," declared Noah as an army of rainbow griefers marched toward them.

8
CLUES

Reenergized from the potion of Healing, Violet rushed toward the griefers with her diamond sword and demanded, "Tell us where Daniel is hiding!"

"Why? He wouldn't bother wasting his time destroying an ordinary townsperson like yourself," an orange griefer replied with a laugh.

"Daniel knows who we are," Violet warned as she inched her way toward the griefer, pointing her sword at his face.

The griefer laughed again. "I know who you are, Violet. So does Daniel. You are just a menace like one of the many hostile mobs in the Overworld. Soon you'll be destroyed. Daniel set your friends to Hardcore mode once before and he's not afraid to do it again."

"We won't let you destroy the Overworld," Violet shouted. One by one, her friends stood behind Violet and pointed their diamond swords at the orange griefer.

"Daniel is still upset that you stole his enchanted book and destroyed his palace. You will have to pay for those crimes." The orange griefer looked back at his army.

Before the griefer could signal his comrades to attack Violet and her friends, she yelled, "Crimes? I freed an entire town from his evil ways. He was controlling everyone with fear. And I didn't steal that book. I found it. Daniel doesn't own every valuable item in the Overworld."

"You underestimate Daniel," the griefer replied as he took out his diamond sword and held it next to Violet's sword. "And you probably underestimate my sword skills. I'm the most skilled fighter in the Overworld. I will defeat you and then when you respawn in that house, the griefers will capture you and set you to Hardcore mode."

Hannah stepped in between Violet and the orange griefer. "Why do bad guys always divulge their plans? Maybe next time you should keep your evil ideas to yourself!" Hannah splashed a potion of Harming and Slowness on the orange griefer, as Violet struck him repeatedly with her diamond sword until he was destroyed.

"I guess he wasn't such a great fighter," concluded Violet. But there was no time for critiques. The griefer army was enraged and rushed toward the gang with great force.

Hannah splashed a potion of Weakness on the griefers as they unleashed their arrows and swords at the gang.

Violet fought with her sword and Hannah stood next to her, splashing the griefers with as many potions as she could throw at this awful army.

The group was winning the battle, but this was just a small feat. They needed to find Daniel. He was hiding somewhere in the Overworld. They had to stop him from staging another attack.

As Violet lunged toward one of the remaining griefers, she saw another griefer holding a shovel and carrying snowballs.

"Here's a clue!" she called out to her friends, but they were still immersed in their battle against the griefers.

"Help!" Noah cried out as he was struck several times by a green griefer.

Violet rushed to Noah. She swung her sword at the green griefer and demanded, "Tell me. Tell me if Daniel is in the Cold Taiga Biome!"

"Never," the green griefer said as Violet thrashed him.

"I know he's in a cold biome," Violet said, and she destroyed the green griefer with her sword.

"Why do you believe Daniel is in a snowy biome?" asked Noah while he struck an orange griefer with his sword.

"I saw a griefer with a shovel and some snowballs. They must have come from that biome," Violet said as she helped Noah finish off the orange griefer.

Harrison looked down at the red griefer he was battling with his diamond sword and saw a patch of snow from a dropped snowball. "You're right Violet! I see snow!"

"You'll never find Daniel," the red griefer called out as Harrison delivered a final blow.

"I think we know where we'll find him," Violet told the group, as they destroyed the last few griefers in the jungle.

When the battle was finished, the group feasted on chicken, cake, and milk they shared from their inventories. As they ate, Violet said, "We have to figure out a plan before we head to the Cold Taiga Biome. I don't want Daniel putting any of us on Hardcore mode. I couldn't bear to see one of us totally destroyed."

"But what if he does capture one of us?" Ben asked nervously as he took a bite of chicken.

"I think it's a chance we have to take," Noah said as he looked out at the horizon. He could see the snowy mountain. His heart sunk and he felt a lump growing in his throat.

"We are in this together. We're going to defeat Daniel," Violet told them. She wanted to believe they'd win this battle, but she had to be honest with herself. She didn't know if that would happen.

The group finished their meals. They looked back at the small house they had created in the jungle and knew they couldn't stay there any longer; they had to move forward.

They traveled through the Ice Plains Biome and past a Frozen River Biome. Violet felt a chill rush through her body. She didn't want to end up on Hardcore mode. With each step through the Ice Plains Biome, she worried about what would happen once they reached Daniel. But she knew she couldn't focus on the fear of fighting Daniel; she had to come up with a good strategy. Once she and her friends had a proper strategy in place, they'd have an advantage over Daniel.

"We need to think of a master plan," Violet said to her friends as they walked slowly and carefully over a thick frozen river.

"I think fighting Daniel is as challenging as walking over this frozen lake," declared Noah. "If we don't take our time and go slowly, we'll fall in and get very hurt."

"Yes," Violet agreed. "And I think you just gave me a good idea for a plan."

9
FROZEN MOUNTAIN

"**W**hat's the plan?" questioned Ben. His heart beat fast as they approached the mountain.

Ferns grew from the snow-covered ground and a wolf loped past the group, frightening them.

"Don't tame it!" warned Violet. "We can't have a dog now."

The group let the wolf run past. Harrison asked, "Violet, what's the plan?"

Violet picked snow up from the ground. "First we should craft some snowballs and place them in our inventory."

Then Violet looked at the group and said, "The plan . . ." she paused. "Once we find Daniel we can't let him know we are all here. We're going to have to split up and surprise him."

Although the plan was relatively basic, the group agreed it was a good starting point. And if they didn't find Daniel's hiding place, they'd never be able to stop him from carrying out his next attack. Ben said in a worried tone, "What if Daniel summoned another Ender Dragon while we were away?"

"I worry about that, too," Violet replied as she inspected the base of the mountain for any holes that might indicate an entrance to a cave where Daniel might have set up his new frozen headquarters.

The gang explored the area surrounding the mountain, but it was only filled with snow and ice. There weren't any caves or igloos.

"I don't think we have time to climb up the mountain," Noah said as he looked at the sky. "We have to build shelter."

Although Violet was focused on finding Daniel, she had to admit she was excited to construct an igloo. She gathered snow and instructed the group on how to build a large igloo. When the snowy home was finished, Violet stared at it. "It's so disappointing that we only get to stay here for one night. We did a really good job."

The sun was setting as the gang entered the icy structure and began to craft beds for the night. Violet heard a rustling noise.

"I think there's someone outside," Violet told her friends and hurried toward the door.

"I don't want you going out there alone," said Noah.

The gang followed Violet outside. Ben lit a torch and placed it by the entrance of the house.

As a creeper approached the igloo, Harrison shot an arrow at the green explosive beast.

Kaboom! The creeper exploded.

Violet said determinedly, "We need to find out where that noise was coming from. It obviously wasn't the creeper."

Exhausted, cold, and nervous, the gang walked farther from the igloo and into the dark, frozen biome.

Harrison said in a quiet whisper, "Guys, I think I see something orange."

The group huddled behind a large snow-covered tree and watched an orange griefer in the distance. He was running away from a gang of skeletons who were hard to see because they were camouflaged by the white snow.

The orange griefer looked over at the group and instead of attacking them, he called out, "Please, help me!"

"Should we?" Elias asked his friends. "Do you think this is a trap?"

"There's only one way to find out," Violet declared. She headed toward the orange griefer and shot an arrow at the skeletons.

The gang followed Violet and battled the bony beasts with diamond swords and arrows. The skeletons dropped bones and bows. The gang gathered the dropped items and placed them in their inventory.

"Thank you," the orange griefer told the gang.

"Who are you?" asked Noah.

"I'm lost." The griefer looked at them and asked, "But you guys look very familiar. Do I know you from somewhere?"

"Your evil leader took over our village, but we were able to defeat him. Now he is staging new attacks," Violet said in one breath.

"Yes! I know who you guys are. Daniel doesn't like you at all." The orange griefer's energy levels were low and he had very little resources left. "I'm running low on energy. Do you have any food you can give me?"

Violet was shocked at how pleasant the griefer was acting. He didn't behave like an enemy, but like a new friend.

"How can we help *you*? You work for one of the worst people in the Overworld," Hannah said as she pointed her diamond sword at the orange man.

"Please don't hurt me," he pleaded. "It's not my fault. I don't even want to be a griefer. Daniel forced me into it."

"Why should we believe you?" demanded Violet.

The orange griefer handed his diamond sword to Violet. "Please take this," he said. "This will prove that I have no bad intentions. I just need a place to sleep."

Violet looked at her friends. She wasn't sure what they should do. She held the diamond sword ready in her hand and excused herself. "I need to consult my friends first."

Each offered their opinion. Hannah said, "I don't think it's a good idea."

Ben said, "We ought to trust him. He handed Violet his sword."

Harrison suggested, "Let's check through his inventory."

And Elias questioned, "What can he do to us?"

Lastly, Noah summed up the situation. "He's vital to us. He probably knows where Daniel is hiding. If he really doesn't want to work for Daniel anymore, maybe he can help us battle him. We need to trust this orange griefer. He's our only lead and we need all the help we can get."

Violet agreed with Noah. The others weren't one hundred percent sold on the idea of having an orange griefer sleep in the igloo, but they all had to admit that Noah was right. They needed to find Daniel, and this stranger could tell them what the griefers were planning.

Violet returned to the orange griefer. "Do you have a name?"

"Funny, nobody ever asks me that. I am just called soldier. But before I became a rainbow soldier, I was a farmer and my name was Jack."

"Well, we're going to call you Jack," Violet announced pleasantly.

"Does that mean you'll let me stay with you guys?" asked Jack.

"Yes, but we need to check through your inventory," she informed him.

"Okay, you can do that!"

Violet paused. ". . . And you have to help us find Daniel."

"I can do that, too!. I don't want to belong to his army anymore!" The orange griefer raised his voice so the rest of the group could hear him.

Violet and her friends let Jack, the orange griefer, into their igloo. They crafted a bed for Jack. They all pulled the wool covers over their bodies and hoped that Jack was being sincere. As the friends drifted off to sleep, they wondered what the new day would bring.

They didn't expect the day to start with a knock on the door.

10
GATHERING FACTS

"**W**ho can that be?" Violet jumped from the bed. She looked over at Jack, the orange griefer. He was still in bed.

"If these are your rainbow griefer friends ready to attack us, you are going to pay, Jack," Ben threatened.

Noah hurried to answer the knock. With his diamond sword in hand, he opened it slowly.

"Angela!" Noah was surprised to see their old friend from the town.

"How did you find us here?" asked Violet.

"It wasn't easy. But I found out from a rainbow griefer that Daniel was in the Cold Taiga Biome and I knew you'd be here. I'm so happy this is your igloo."

"What rainbow griefer?" questioned Ben.

"They're back. Kyle and I spotted one in town. We captured the griefer and got some information. He was sent there to blow up as many structures as he could." Angela gave them the details of the capture and told them how the desperate, trapped griefer alerted her to Daniel's location and his plan to summon the Wither on the town.

"Yes, he is planning on summoning the Wither," the orange griefer confirmed.

"Who is this? Why do you have a rainbow griefer staying with you?" Angela was confused.

"We captured him last night," Hannah told her.

"His name is Jack and he doesn't want to be a griefer anymore," explained Violet.

"Daniel calls us all soldiers," the orange griefer clarified. "We don't get to have individual names."

"It doesn't matter what you call yourself. You are just a bunch of bullies who cause trouble and hurt innocent people," Harrison told Jack.

Violet didn't want the gang to get distracted in a debate about whether Jack was a griefer or a soldier; she wanted to save her town and stop Daniel before he called in the Wither. "When is he summoning the Wither?" she asked.

"I'm not sure, but he wants to do it soon. He was trying to figure out the command blocks to summon the Wither," confessed Jack.

"We have to stop him! Where is he hiding?" Hannah took out her sword and pointed the weapon at Jack.

"There's no need to point swords," Violet admonished as she reached for Hannah's sword. "We should be nice to each other. We all have the same plan. We want to defeat Daniel."

"Yes, I want to defeat Daniel, too," exclaimed Jack.

"Great, then we are on the same page," Hannah said, but she didn't believe him. She wanted to get as much information out of him as they could before he turned on them.

The gang ate apples and drank milk because they needed strength to battle Daniel. After they were done eating, they followed Jack down a snowy path.

"Daniel was staying here," said Jack, and he led them to a large hole on the side of a mountain.

The group carefully and quietly entered the cave. Violet walked closely behind Jack. "The cave is empty," she called out.

"They must know you are looking for them," Jack speculated as he examined the cave.

There was a large hole in the ground. Ben looked down and said, "It looks like they were mining here."

Elias shouted, "Blue! I see blue! There are diamonds here." He was about to climb into the hole with his pickaxe in hand, but Violet warned him to stop.

"This could be a trap. I don't trust Daniel. Why would he leave a cave with diamonds?" Violet looked around the entrance.

"Look, there's a room with empty beds," Ben yelled to the gang.

"Evidently they're coming back," surmised Violet. "They didn't abandon the cave; they're probably out hunting for us."

"What are we going to do? Should we leave?" Ben's voice quavered. He was very nervous.

"No, we are staying," declared Violet.

Hannah put on her helmet, grabbed her pickaxe, and jumped into the hole. "I'm mining while they are away. I want diamonds."

Ben joined Hannah, and the two mined for diamonds.

"I think someone should watch out for Daniel," suggested Noah.

Jack volunteered. "I think I should be the watchman, because I blend in."

The group spread out in different directions around the frozen cave. Elias walked down a long hall and investigated various rooms. Angela searched the main room. They were all looking for any clues that could help them figure out what other attacks Daniel was staging.

Violet entered a room with only one bed. "This must be Daniel's room," she called out to Noah, who followed her into the room.

"A chest!" Noah raced to look it over.

Noah and Violet opened the chest. It was filled with numerous enchanted books.

"If he has so many enchanted books, why was he focused on finding the one that I had taken from that cave?" Violet questioned.

"It looks like he collects them. Maybe he wants all of the enchanted books in the Overworld."

Violet thought Noah's analysis made sense, but she also wondered if Daniel wanted the books because he was planning some master attack that involved a battle with multiple enchanted swords.

The group explored the rest of his room, but there was nothing there to help them figure out his next move.

Disappointed, Violet and Noah walked out of the room. Noah's heart skipped a beat when he heard Jack shout, "They're here!"

11
HIDE AND SEEK

"Jump down here!" Hannah hollered up from the hole. "It looks like there's a stronghold. We can hide there."

Harrison, Elias, Angela, Violet, and Noah emerged from rooms deep within the icy cave and quickly jumped into the hole where Hannah and Ben were mining.

It was a race against time. When they finally reached the bottom of the hole, they could hear Daniel and the rainbow griefers returning. Hannah led them safely to a door, but as they opened the door to the stronghold, they could hear a rainbow griefer state, "Wow, I don't remember digging that deep. I'm a better miner than I thought."

The gang rushed through the entrance and into the stronghold before the griefers could spot them. They found themselves in a large empty room. Noah noted as he walked down the hall, "Sometimes there's treasure in a stronghold."

"I'm worried that we'll end up t-t-trapped here. How are we going to get out when Daniel and the rainbow griefers are above us?" Ben stuttered as he spoke.

"There's no turning back now." Noah led them down the hall and into a room that had two floors and a cobblestone center.

"It's a storeroom," remarked Violet as she looked at the torch and walked up the wooden stairs to the second floor, where she discovered a treasure chest.

"Look! She found a chest!" Elias exclaimed as he followed behind Violet.

Violet opened the chest. "More enchanted books!" she said in excitement.

"Daniel would go crazy if he knew you had his chest of enchanted books," added Noah.

The group placed the enchanted books in their inventories.

"Watch out!" yelled Harrison.

A silverfish crawled past them. Noah reached for his diamond sword and struck the insect.

"Look over there!" Ben shouted.

The group watched a huge group of silverfish crawl into the storeroom.

"There has to be a spawner nearby," said Noah as he dashed toward the silverfish and tried to strike as many as he could with his sword.

The others joined Noah in his battle against the small bugs. Violet ran past the insects on a quest to find the spawner in the stronghold. As she raced down the hall, she was struck with an arrow.

"Ouch!" Violet called out. She looked up to see three skeletons standing in front of her, pointing their bows and arrows at her. Violet was outnumbered. She lashed out at a skeleton, but the others shot arrows at her. "Help!" Violet called to her friends.

Hannah was the first one to help Violet clobber the bony menaces. She also used her diamond sword to attack the skeletons, but they were strong and the battle wasn't easy.

"Somebody help us!" Hannah yelled as she saw more skeletons marching down the hall toward them.

Click. Clack. Clang. Their bones clanged as they advanced toward Violet and Hannah.

The two friends struck many of the skeletons, but they weren't making any progress. These skilled bony fighters were able to inflict damage on both warriors, despite all the armor they wore. They needed help.

With a sword in one hand, Hannah was able to grab a bottle of a splash potion of Healing. She splashed it on two skeletons. They were destroyed and dropped bones.

Elias, Ben, and Angela rushed to join them in battle. They struck as many skeletons as they could, and they felt confident that they'd win the battle until Noah hollered, "Help us! This room is flooded with zombies and silverfish."

"Do you think this is a trap?" Violet questioned as she struck another skeleton and worried that her energy level was about to be depleted.

Angela raced down the hall to help Noah. Violet felt powerless; she couldn't help them because she was barely handling her own battle.

Angela called out, "I found the silverfish spawner. Someone help me deactivate it!"

Ben ran to Angela's side. Violet felt relieved that at least one of the mobs was being destroyed.

Hannah's potion of Healing was destroying the skeletons faster than a strike from a sword. She kept splashing the potion while Violet finished off the weakened skeletons with a strike from her sword.

"We make a good team," Hannah said as she splashed more potions on the skeletons.

"Yes, but we have to save some of that potion for ourselves. We are losing too much energy in this battle." Violet tried to catch her breath as she struck the final skeleton.

When the final bone dropped to the ground, Noah shouted again, "Violet, I need you!" Violet and Hannah dashed down the hall. They weren't prepared for the battle they were about to fight. The room was filled with vacant-eyed zombies. There were so many zombies that it was almost impossible to move around.

"This is crazy. I've never seen this many zombies in one place before. This has to be one of Daniel's attacks." Violet struck a zombie, but another hit her, and she lost energy.

"We can do this!" Noah told them as he threw a potion of Healing on the zombies and weakened the walking dead beasts.

"There are too many to battle!" yelled Violet. She charged three zombies with her sword, striking them as hard as she could, but only destroyed one.

Ben and Harrison were battling zombies that were wearing armor, and they were about to lose the battle.

Violet worried they'd be destroyed and respawn in the igloo, where Daniel would be waiting to capture them and put them on Hardcore mode.

Hannah shouted, "Everyone take out all the potions you have that can harm the zombies and throw them at these beasts."

The group followed Hannah's direction and the zombies were all destroyed.

"Excellent!" Noah shouted in relief.

"An extreme splash attack!" Violet praised her friend, "Good idea, Hannah!"

They wanted to celebrate. Everyone grabbed milk and potions of Healing from their inventories to regain their strength. It was a jubilant time, but it was also very brief. Once the group finished their drinks, they heard a voice call out to them from below the storeroom.

"Are you ready for another battle?" the voice asked with a sinister laugh.

12
BACK TO THE END

"It's Daniel!" Harrison shouted. The group rushed down the hall in search of an exit from the stronghold.

"How are we going to get out of here? I knew it! We're trapped!" Ben called out to the group.

"Down here!" Violet turned into a room at the end of the hall.

"Not again!" Noah sighed.

The rainbow griefers could be heard in the hallway, while the group stared at a portal in the middle of the room.

"We have to go to the End. It's our only way out," Noah said. He jumped on the portal and activated it.

"I don't want to go to the End!" Angela was terrified; she had never been to the End before.

"It's our only choice," Noah called out. "Come quickly."

The group joined Noah on the portal and within seconds they were in the End, and standing in front of a large Ender Dragon that roared in their faces.

Violet threw a snowball at the Ender Dragon, but that only aggravated it.

Noah tried to strike it with his sword, but missed and was hit by the Ender Dragon, depleting his health.

"We have to destroy the Ender crystals," Noah told his friends. "That's our best chance at winning this battle."

Harrison aimed at the Ender crystals but missed them. A swarm of Endermites approached him. He tried to strike as many as he could with his sword. "Help!" he cried out.

Violet looked down in disgust at the Endermite invasion, as the Ender Dragon swiftly flew down from the sky and struck her with its powerful wing.

"Ugh!" she cried as her energy ran dangerously low.

Violet rallied her remaining bit of energy to strike the dragon again. Hannah stood by her friend, throwing snowballs at the dragon.

Elias helped Harrison battle the Endermites. There were hundreds of small Endermites crawling around the ground and attacking them. Ben joined them and destroyed a bunch of the Endermites. He called out, "Look up!"

Gangs of Endermen had spawned and were teleporting toward them. There was nowhere to hide. The group had a dragon flying at them from above, and Endermites and Endermen were attacking them on the ground.

An Enderman shrieked and teleported next to Ben, striking him. He was destroyed. Violet glanced over and noticed that Ben had disappeared. She worried he'd spawn in the igloo and Daniel would put him on Hardcore mode. She couldn't concentrate on the battle. The Ender

Dragon swooped down and roared at Violet, but she bravely struck the flying evil creature with her sword.

Hannah shot an arrow at the Ender Crystals and they exploded. Angela hit the other Ender crystals, but it was too late. The explosion didn't damage the dragon and thus it couldn't save Violet. She was respawned back into the igloo.

As Violet woke up in the bed in the igloo, she saw her friends respawn, one by one, into the frozen home.

"We're all here!" She was relieved and said, "And Daniel isn't even here! We're safe."

Noah looked around at the others. "We're not all here. Ben is missing!"

"I wonder if Daniel captured him," Violet thought aloud in a worried tone.

There was a knock on the door and Violet hurried to open it. It was Jack, the orange griefer.

"Where's Ben?" demanded Violet.

"Ben? I have no idea. But I have big news for you," Jack said as he entered the igloo.

"We don't want your news, we want to find our friend. We know your evil leader captured him. He could be on Hardcore mode at this very minute and could be destroyed." Harrison pointed his sword menacingly at Jack.

"Daniel doesn't have Jack. He is too busy summoning the Wither to your town. He finally figured out the command blocks. And he also sent a small group of rainbow griefers to blow up your tree house," confessed Jack.

Suddenly Ben walked into the igloo.

"Where were you?" Violet was angry. She couldn't believe he'd simply left the igloo and hadn't waited for the others to respawn. They were in this together and had promised to wait for each other before they left the respawning point.

"I heard a noise outside. I was worried it was Daniel," Ben told them, "I didn't know what to do."

The group forgave Ben, but they didn't have time for any discussions. They had to make their way back to the town and they had to do it fast. The gang quickly ate some food and checked through their inventories to make sure they had enough supplies for the trip back to the village.

Jack asked, "Can I come with you guys?"

Harrison blurted out, "Does he have to? I don't trust him."

Violet was upset with Harrison. "That's not nice. We should trust him. He just gave us this valuable information."

Noah looked at Jack and said, "Of course you're welcome to join us. You're our friend."

The group left the igloo. They wanted to get back to the town as fast as they could, but they knew the journey wouldn't be easy.

"We have to stop the griefers! They can't scare the townspeople with the Wither!" Harrison called out.

"And they'd better not ruin my tree house." Violet was enraged. She had worked very hard to craft that tree house and would be devastated if the house was destroyed.

The group trekked through the snowy biome into the jungle. As they approached an area thick with leaves and giant trees, arrows shot toward them.

"Rainbow griefers!" Violet shouted.

The gang took out their swords and bows and arrows as the sky grew cloudy and rain began to fall on the green jungle.

Three blue griefers lunged toward the gang, but were struck by arrows.

"Skeletons!" one of the blue griefers screamed to his friends.

But the other two griefers weren't paying attention to their friend's warning about the skeleton attack. They stared at Jack the orange griefer. They held their diamond swords against his orange body. "Traitor," one of the blue griefers shouted at Jack and struck him with a diamond sword.

"How can we be betrayed by one of our own people?" the other blue griefer asked as he too struck Jack.

Arrows shot through the sky, hitting all three blue griefers. The gang took shelter behind a large jungle tree.

"We have to help Jack," Violet said as she peeked out from behind the tree and saw her friend being attacked.

"You're right," Noah agreed, holding his sword tightly in his hand. He was eager to battle the blue griefers.

As Noah and Violet ran to help their friends, the skeletons destroyed the three blue griefers.

"You're safe! The blue griefers are wiped out," Violet called out to Jack.

Jack turned around and lunged at the skeletons with his sword. Noah and Violet joined him in battle, as the sun began to break through the clouds and the skeletons were destroyed.

"We have to get moving," Ben called out. "I see more rainbow griefers in the distance."

13
IT TAKES A VILLAGE

The gang raced to outrun the griefers, but the evil creatures were catching up to them. "We have to go faster!" Violet called to her friends.

"I can't go any faster," Noah replied wearily.

The town was in sight. They could see the golem outside the village shops. "We're almost there," Ben said. He was happy to see the golem.

Night was setting in as the group reached the village street, stopping to catch a breath by Valentino's butcher shop.

Valentino saw the group and came out of his shop. "I'm so glad to see you. The town is being attacked again. This morning somebody blew up a farm and the blacksmith shop. I am so worried my butcher shop will be blown up. Then I won't have a place to sell my goods."

"We're trying to stop it, but we need help," replied Noah.

Valentino spotted Jack the orange griefer. "What is an orange griefer doing in our village? He can't stay here. He's the enemy."

"No, Valentino. He's our friend," Violet defended Jack.

Violet went up and down the village streets recruiting townspeople to help them battle the rainbow griefers that were about to enter the town. She also asked them to be kind to Jack, and explained that he was now on their side and would help them with the battle.

"Everyone," she announced to the townspeople, "we need your help. We have to battle these rainbow griefers and we can't do it without you. Go home and suit up in armor and then come back and help us with your powerful swords and bows and arrows."

The townspeople rushed back to their homes so they could help the gang battle the griefers that were intent on destroying their town. But some townspeople stopped and protested, "How can you bring an orange griefer into our town? How can you trust him?"

"Please," Violet said, trying to be patient, "leave Jack alone. He is our friend."

The sky grew darker. Harrison lit a torch and placed it on the side of Valentino's shop.

Violet called out to the crowd, "We're losing valuable time. We don't have time to argue about Jack. You'll see. He will join us in battle."

The rainbow griefers walked past the golem. The gang advanced toward them, ready to battle.

Jack was the first to strike a griefer.

"I can't believe I was struck by one of my own," cried the griefer.

"I'm not like you anymore," Jack shouted and attacked him again.

The townspeople began to crowd the village streets and join the gang in battle.

Ben struck one griefer with his sword, but another griefer clobbered him, destroying him.

"Oh no!" Hannah was devastated. "He's going to respawn in the igloo."

With a surge of anger, she struck the griefer and instantly obliterated him. The gang, along with many townspeople, destroyed all the griefers that were attacking their village. It was a thrilling victory and the entire town was pleased. But it was still the dead of night and they were all vulnerable to hostile mob attacks.

"Everybody can go to sleep now," instructed Violet. "We heard that Daniel is summoning the Wither. We must get some rest and prepare for the battle. Thank you for helping us today! We will beat Daniel again and win!"

Everyone headed back home. Hannah stopped Violet and Noah. "Where are you going?"

"We have to sleep before the morning. We need to restore our energy to battle Daniel," replied Violet.

"What? How can you go to bed when Ben was destroyed? He probably respawned in the igloo; Daniel could have captured him and put him on Hardcore mode. He must be so frightened. You know he isn't that brave. He tries, but he isn't really made for battle," Hannah reminded her friends.

Angela, Elias, and Harrison agreed with Hannah. Even though it was pitch black and they could be destroyed by the hostile mobs of the night, they had to trek through the darkness to save their friend Ben.

Violet added, "I'm also worried about Ben, but we have to stay and get some sleep. We need to defend this town."

"I thought we were in this together," Jack the orange griefer said to Violet.

Violet took his words to heart. She wondered if she was making the wrong decision. Was her determination to save the town stopping her from doing the right thing?

Noah looked over at Violet. "They're right. We can't leave Ben in the Cold Taiga Biome alone. He might be captured."

"What are we going to do?" Hannah asked the group.

"We're going to split up," replied Violet.

As a group of zombies lumbered toward the town, Noah shot an arrow at one of the beasts.

"No, we aren't splitting up," Noah disagreed firmly, as he fought the zombies with his friends. "We're going to save Ben together."

Violet aimed at a zombie and struck it with her arrow. She didn't realize four zombies were lurking behind her. Within seconds she was destroyed and respawned in the igloo. There sat Daniel.

14
SMALL WONDER

"**W**here is Ben?" Violet confronted Daniel immediately.

"Your friend will be okay," he said with a laugh.

Seconds later, Noah respawned in the igloo. He dashed toward Daniel, striking him with his diamond sword. But two rainbow griefers lunged at Noah and his sword broke, leaving him defenseless.

"It's time for you to pay," Daniel exclaimed as he looked at Noah and Violet. "You destroyed my palace and stole my enchanted books, and you stole diamonds from my mine."

"You summoned the Ender Dragon to attack our town and hurt innocent people. And you stole that palace. I built it for a friend of mine and you took it from them," Violet replied. Her eyes started to fill with tears. "And what have you done with Ben?"

Violet felt very guilty. If something happened to Ben, she would blame herself for hesitating to rescue him.

"You guys are going back to my ice cave and you will be placed on Hardcore mode." Daniel let out a sinister laugh.

Harrison and Hannah had respawned in their beds. They jumped up and struck the griefers in the room, but it didn't have any impact. More griefers came in the door of the igloo. The friends were outnumbered. Daniel controlled the Cold Taiga Biome and they were going to have to fight to survive.

Elias respawned in his bed too, and a red griefer was already standing by the bed waiting for him. Finally, Jack the orange griefer respawned.

Daniel walked over to him and asked, "How can you join these people? You're one of us."

"He isn't one of us, he's an evil traitor and he must be destroyed," said the red griefer. "It would be my pleasure if you let me destroy this piece of trash."

"Don't do anything rash," Daniel replied as he held a diamond sword to Jack the orange griefer's face. "I want to deal with him myself. This one needs special attention. He'll be the first to be placed on Hardcore mode."

"You aren't going to get away with this!" Violet shouted at Daniel, but she wasn't sure she was right about that. She knew Daniel could destroy them all. After spending so much time trying to save the townspeople, Violet knew the townspeople were their only hope of being saved. If the townspeople could make it to this cold biome and fight Daniel and his griefers, the gang might be saved. If not, Violet and her friends would be put on Hardcore mode, and even the most skilled fighter can be destroyed on that mode. It's not just a challenge, it's impossible.

Violet and her friends did something they never thought they'd do. They surrendered.

"We will go back to your ice cave. Please, just don't hurt us." Violet spoke for her friends. "And please let us see Ben."

"Ben is fine," Daniel laughed. "Don't worry about him."

It was still dark and the group walked alongside the rainbow griefers through the snow toward the ice cave.

Although the cave was close to the igloo, Violet felt like the walk took forever. Each step felt like an eternity. She looked over at Noah and hoped he had a plan to escape, because she had nothing. The others walked with their heads down. Everyone was frightened and cold.

The griefers led them down the hole they had used to mine for diamonds and into the stronghold. They walked down the hall and were led into a prison cell. The group gathered in a small cell, where they were reunited with Ben.

One of the griefers closed the gate. Daniel looked at them from behind the bars and let out another sinister laugh. "Well, you're reunited with your friend Ben. I told you he was okay."

The group stared back at Daniel, unafraid of his evil threats.

"Your days are numbered. You're all trapped. Who is going to save you now?" Daniel laughed again.

"You'll never win," Violet shouted from behind the bars.

"Really? I won't?" Daniel taunted, "because it looks like I have already won. You're all my prisoners. And soon you will be on Hardcore mode and I'll be rid of you."

"This is cruel and you're not being fair to anybody, Daniel," Jack the orange griefer called out.

Daniel signaled to the green griefers that stood next to him to remove Jack from the cell, and they walked toward the cell to take him away.

"Don't listen to him," Jack told them. "Don't trust him. He doesn't care about you. He'd destroy you in minutes. I'd rather be destroyed with the people next to me in this cell than live a life working for somebody like Daniel."

"Well, I can grant you that wish," Daniel shouted at Jack.

A red griefer sprinted down the hall and whispered something in Daniel's ear. He told the green griefers to leave Jack in the prison cell and left in a hurry. Once he was gone, Hannah asked, "How are we going to get out of here?"

"You're not," one of the green griefers replied.

"You don't scare us," Violet called to the griefers.

"We should scare you," the green griefer said as he approached the cell.

Two silverfish crawled toward the green griefers, who hit them with their swords. But they were so busy battling the small insects they didn't see the creeper that silently crept behind them and ignited itself.

Kaboom!

The creeper destroyed one of the green griefers. The other was left alone with dozens of silverfish crawling toward him. He hit as many as he could with his sword, but it was a silverfish infestation and there were too many to battle.

"Do you need help?" asked Violet.

"Not from you," the griefer replied as he struck another silverfish. And the green griefer was also so distracted by the insects that he didn't see a skeleton in the distance. It shot an arrow at the green griefer and he was destroyed.

"We have to get out of here!" Violet tried to break out from behind the bars. Together the gang ripped the bars down, and they were free.

"Let's find Daniel!" Noah raced down the hall.

The gang had renewed energy. They could win the battle after all. They ran down the hall in search of Daniel. When they climbed out of the hole in the middle of the ice cave, they heard a familiar voice.

15
EXPECTATIONS

"**A**ngela!" Violet called out.

"I'm going to save you!" Angela replied.

Violet looked behind Angela and saw a large group of townspeople. They were dressed in armor and carried diamond swords and bows and arrows.

"Where's Daniel?" Noah asked Angela.

"I have no idea. There's nobody here," Angela replied.

Violet walked into the empty ice cave. There was no sign of Daniel and the griefers.

"Where did they go?" Harrison wondered as he inspected the rooms of the ice cave.

"I don't know, but we're going to find out." Violet was determined to stop Daniel.

The gang dashed out of the ice cave, and the townspeople followed them through the frigid snow-covered biome in search of Daniel and the griefers.

"I see them!" Noah called to the group. In the distance, the rainbow griefers were entering the Jungle Biome.

"To the jungle!" directed Violet.

The gang headed toward the jungle, but once they reached the leafy biome, they didn't see any of the griefers.

"How did we lose them?" asked Violet, who was visibly annoyed. She looked in every direction, but there was no trace of Daniel and his evil army.

"What about the jungle temple?" Noah asked as he pointed to the temple in the distance.

"We can check there," Violet said and led the way toward the temple.

Violet looked behind her, noticing a large group of townspeople. She felt powerful leading the townspeople to the jungle, but she was also nervous. She didn't feel like a born leader, and she wasn't comfortable having so many villagers follow her. Violet also had no great plan for when they reached Daniel and the griefers. If they were in the temple, she'd just attack them with her sword. She knew that she needed a strategy to defeat the griefers.

Jack walked along behind Violet. "Daniel has another hiding place in the jungle. It's a cave near the jungle temple."

"Thanks," said Violet. "Can you lead us there?"

"Yes," he replied and moved to the front of the line, side by side with Violet.

"Do they have any weak spots in the cave? Anything you can tell us to help win this battle?" questioned Violet as she tried to come up with a strategy.

"The cave is very similar to the ice cave," he replied. "It also has a large stronghold."

Violet was nervous they'd be stuck in a stronghold again and would have to travel back to the End.

"Maybe we should just head back to the town and protect it?" Violet questioned.

Noah walked over to them and Jack told him about the jungle cave.

"We have to invade the cave. It can weaken the griefers and help us win this battle," decided Noah.

Violet knew Noah was right. They continued past the jungle temple and toward the cave, when the sky turned dark and it started to rain.

"Ouch!" Noah called out.

Arrows were suddenly flying in all directions and hitting the gang.

"Skeletons!" shouted Harrison.

The group took out their swords and bows and arrows and began to battle the bony mob.

The sound of rattling bones could be heard in the jungle, as Violet and her friends tried to defeat the mob as fast as they could, without depleting all of their energy. They needed to stay strong to battle Daniel.

Click! Clack! Clang! A skeleton shot an arrow that pierced Violet's skin. Violet lunged toward the skeleton with a diamond sword, but she was shocked when someone struck her back with a powerful diamond sword.

"You can't even fight a skeleton," Daniel taunted, and he struck Violet again.

Violet was cornered. She didn't know whom to fight. She had Daniel at her back as she stood face to face with a skeleton.

"Violet!" Noah called out, "Don't worry about the skeleton." He shot an arrow at the bony beast and it was destroyed.

"Daniel, where's your army?" Violet pointed her sword directly at Daniel.

"I don't need them to battle you. It's very easy," he laughed.

As Daniel let out another sinister chuckle, Violet struck him with her sword. He became very angry and fought back.

The gang surrounded Daniel and Violet. They were ready to destroy Daniel when they saw the rainbow griefers marching into their town.

"Your town is going to be destroyed," Daniel laughed again, as he drank a potion of Healing to regain his energy.

The townspeople rushed to the rainbow griefers, flooding them with arrows and trying to strike them with their swords. But the skeletons were advancing toward both the griefers and the townspeople.

The rainbow griefers and the townspeople had to work together to fight off the group of skeletons that attacked them in the rain. Yet, they didn't bond during the battle. Once the last skeleton was defeated and dropped a bone, the rainbow griefers and the townspeople continued with their battle, until finally the rain stopped and the sun began to shine throughout the town.

Violet kept her sword aimed at Daniel. "Why are you doing this to us? Can't you leave our town alone?"

"Never!" he laughed. "I won't be happy until it's destroyed!"

Noah shot an arrow at Daniel. Harrison, Angela, Kyle, Ben, and Hannah raced toward Daniel with their swords. He was outnumbered. But he did something very unusual. He quickly took off his armor and then grabbed a potion from his inventory. Within a second, he was invisible.

"Ugh!" Hannah cried as she was struck by Daniel's sword.

They tried to hit him, but they couldn't see where he was. The diamond sword wasn't floating through the air. He was gone.

"We need to help the others battle the griefers," Violet said. She hurried over to the townspeople who were engaged in a serious battle against Daniel's enormous colorful army.

A bright blue light flashed in the distance.

"That's coming from the direction of our town!" cried Violet.

The Wither had spawned.

16
TRICKS AND TREATS

Kaboom! An explosion rocked the town.

"We have to go help! Many of the villagers are defenseless," Noah exclaimed as he headed toward the town. He thought about Valentino and his butcher shop.

The townspeople stopped battling the griefers and followed Noah and the others back to the town. As they raced there, they were showered with arrows from the rainbow griefers that were on their trail.

Noah reached the village streets. A black three-headed beast shot a fast-moving black wither skull at Noah, but he dodged the skull and attacked the Wither with an arrow.

The Wither floated through the town unleashing a barrage of wither skulls and striking and destroying many townspeople.

Violet threw a snowball at the Wither, but a blue skull hit her arm and she was struck with the Wither effect.

"I'm so tired," she cried out, "help!"

Hannah rushed over with milk, which cured Violet quickly. Together they tried to battle the Wither with the others, but it was an impossible fight. The three-headed monster terrorized the town with its powerful wither skulls that flew through the air and struck innocent people.

"The town is being destroyed!" Violet cried out. She was upset. The Wither had blown up a few homes and a farm.

The townspeople used everything they could to battle this awful flying beast. They threw snowballs, they shot arrows, and they used their swords to strike the menace when it was flying close to the ground. Yet, nothing worked. The Wither was still full of energy and floating above the town.

"We need to trap it," said Ben.

"But how?" asked Harrison.

"Violet," Ben called to his friend. "You can build an obsidian room and trap it."

"That's a great idea." Violet went through her inventory to find the materials to build an obsidian structure.

Hannah and Noah helped Violet craft the obsidian prison for the Wither, as the others shot arrows at the beast. Harrison hit the Wither with a snowball, and it roared, but its energy level was still high.

As Violet crafted the obsidian structure, night began to set in, and a creeper snuck up behind Noah and exploded.

Kaboom!

"Noah!" Violet shrieked.

The structure was almost complete, but Violet was worried about her friend respawning in the Cold Taiga Biome. She wondered if Daniel had any rainbow griefers waiting there, and if they would put Noah on Hardcore mode.

Some rainbow griefers were still battling townspeople in the village. Violet could see Jack the orange griefer battle a blue griefer off in the distance. This battle seemed almost too intense for Violet. They had to fight the Wither, rainbow griefers, and now they were subject to attacks from the hostile mobs that spawned in the night. She knew she had to fight, but she really wanted to teleport to the cold biome to find Noah. Violet finished the room and told Harrison, "The obsidian room is done. Trap the Wither."

"Aren't you going to help me?" questioned Harrison.

"I have to TP to the igloo. I'm sorry. I can't leave Noah. I have to help him," replied Violet, as she began to teleport to the snowy cold biome.

Violet stood in the igloo. Noah called out, "Violet!"

"We must get back to the village, Noah. We have to trap the Wither!"

Noah and Violet teleported together, landing in the middle of the village streets. A red griefer hit Noah with his sword and Violet struck the evil creature.

"My energy level is low," Noah told Violet. She gave him some milk.

The Wither flew through the town. Harrison and Ben were taunting the Wither and trying to lead it to the obsidian room as two green rainbow griefers charged toward them with their swords out.

Violet shot arrows at the green rainbow griefers, but missed them.

"Watch out!" yelled Noah, as a group of zombies walked into the village and toward Violet.

"How many mobs do we have to battle?" Violet asked with an exhausted sigh.

Noah lunged at the zombies and clobbered them. As he ran back to Violet, a red griefer hit him with a diamond sword. Noah was weakened but he could still run. He wanted to help his friends capture the Wither that terrorized the town.

"I think I hit it!" Noah called out as he shot an arrow at the Wither. It raged loudly and flew toward Noah.

"Keep running toward the obsidian house!" instructed Violet.

"You're almost there," said Ben. "You can do it, Noah!"

Two Endermen carrying bricks spotted Noah as he sprinted toward the obsidian house. One of the Endermen shrieked and teleported next to him. Hannah raced over with a potion and splashed it on the Enderman.

The Wither was flying toward Noah. Harrison, Ben, Kyle, and Angela positioned themselves outside the obsidian house. They planned on flooding the Wither with a sea of arrows to weaken it and then trap the flying menace in the obsidian room.

The Wither approached. The friends unleashed their arrows and the Wither was overwhelmed. Violet lunged at the Wither with her diamond sword. She used great force and was able to get the Wither to fly toward the obsidian house. Noah joined Violet and they struck the Wither together. Hannah threw snowballs at the Wither, as the gang at last trapped the beast in the obsidian room.

"We're saved!" Noah called out.

"I don't think so," Violet said as she looked over at an army of griefers. They all had their weapons aimed at the group. One griefer stood out from the rest. It was Jack the orange griefer. He had his sword pointed at Violet.

"Free the Wither!" shouted a green griefer, but Violet wouldn't respond. She just stared at Jack the orange griefer in disbelief.

17
WATCH YOUR BACK

"**J**ack!" Violet called out. She took out her diamond sword, ready to charge at her friend.

Jack looked at Violet and smiled, and then struck the blue griefer standing next to him.

"Traitor!" one of the pink griefers screamed, and the griefers began to attack Jack.

Noah sprinted to Jack's side to fight the griefers. The rainbow griefers were so busy trying to destroy Jack they weren't paying attention to the crowd of townspeople who ran toward them and attacked. The griefer army was losing soldiers quickly.

"Ouch!" Hannah cried.

She turned around to see a spider jockey standing in front of her. The skeleton riding the red-eyed spider shot arrows at her. Since everyone was busy battling the griefers, nobody noticed Hannah being attacked by the bony beast riding an arachnid. She dodged arrows from the skeleton as she struck the spider with her sword and destroyed it.

An arrow flew from behind Hannah and obliterated the skeleton. She looked over and saw Violet.

"I couldn't let you get destroyed by a spider jockey. We have griefers to destroy and a trapped Wither," Violet said.

The two rushed toward the griefers and joined the others in battle. The griefer army was diminishing. Two pink griefers broke away from the group and headed for the obsidian house.

"Stop them!" Jack called out in a weak voice. He was being attacked by a group of griefers.

Violet and Hannah raced toward the pink griefers, trying to hit them with arrows.

The pink griefers reached the obsidian house and freed the Wither. It flew out and shot wither skulls at the pink griefers, destroying them.

"Isn't that ironic?" remarked Violet.

"We have to get that Wither back into the obsidian house." Hannah shot an arrow at the Wither.

The Wither swooped down toward the rainbow griefers and the townspeople, pelting them with wither skulls. The group was struck with the Wither effect.

Violet and Hannah stood in front of the obsidian house. Violet threw snowballs. Hannah shot arrows. This angered the Wither. It flew toward them in a rage and aimed wither skulls at the two warriors.

"We need help!" Violet called to the others who were still battling the rainbow griefers.

Noah and Harrison ran toward them. They aimed their weapons at the Wither and forced it back into the obsidian room.

The sun was beginning to rise. Hannah looked over at the ongoing battle between the griefers and the townspeople.

"Where's Daniel?" Hannah shouted. Her voice carried throughout the village.

A green griefer stopped. "Why do you ask?"

"If he's so brave and is in control, why doesn't he fight? Every time there is a big battle, he always seems to be missing," Hannah said.

"He is fighting. He's the one who is controlling the Wither." A green griefer defended him.

Hannah pointed to the obsidian house where they had trapped the Wither. "It looks like he's doing a great job, right?" she said sarcastically. "Well, now he's trapped at last."

The griefers paused. They actually stopped battling the townspeople and stood still. Violet was shocked and wondered if they were reconsidering Daniel's behavior.

Hannah continued, "Why are you fighting us? Because Daniel told you to do it?"

There was silence.

"Most of you are getting destroyed and there's no reason for any of this. We all have enough hostile mobs to fight in the Overworld. Why should we battle each other?"

The griefers remained silent.

"Daniel is the one behind all of this evil. If we all work together, we can end his horrible reign of fear and terror."

Jack called out, "How can we do that, Hannah?"

"I ask you all to change your skins to whatever skin you'd like. Don't use the colors of the rainbow, though. If you change your skin, you can stay here. We'll help you build a home and we will give you a new life. A better life. A life where you can be free to make choices and where you can fight your own battles, not battles that an evil dictator forces you to fight." Hannah spoke passionately.

A green griefer stood in front of the group, announcing, "I want to change."

One by one the rainbow griefers began to change their skins. They chose skins with red hair, brown hair, some wore glasses, others wore jumpsuits, but they were all different, and they weren't rainbow griefers anymore.

Within minutes, there weren't any more rainbow griefers. There was just a peaceful town with a new group of residents. The sun seemed to shine brighter, and Hannah offered the new friends food.

"Let's all feast!" she announced.

A townsperson with glasses and a vest walked over to her and said, "Thank you." He smiled.

"I'm so happy everyone listened. This is the best day of my life." Hannah was excited and introduced herself to the newcomer in the vest.

"You don't recognize me?" he asked with a shy grin.

Violet walked over to Hannah and the stranger in the vest. "Hi, Jack!" she called out.

"You're not orange anymore!" Hannah remarked.

"Good job on that speech," Noah complimented Hannah.

Harrison, Ben, Angela, and Kyle also walked over to Hannah to commend her on her persuasive speaking.

"You destroyed the griefer army without fighting," said Violet. She was both inspired and impressed.

"We still have to get rid of the Wither," Ben reminded everyone as he looked at the obsidian house with dread.

Noah gathered blocks of TNT.

"What are you planning to do?" asked Violet.

"I think we should fill the obsidian house with TNT and blow up the Wither," replied Noah as he took the last block of TNT from his inventory.

"Do you need any more TNT?" asked Harrison.

"Yes, we'll need a lot," replied Noah.

"What a great idea!" Violet exclaimed. She looked at the obsidian house she'd built. "Since obsidian doesn't get destroyed by TNT, we'll still have the house after the Wither explodes."

The gang carefully filled the obsidian house with TNT, making sure they didn't let the Wither get free while they placed the blocks of TNT.

Noah used flint and steel, igniting the TNT.

Kaboom!

The Wither was destroyed. There was reason to celebrate in town. Although Daniel was still missing, he had lost his biggest asset, his army of rainbow griefers.

"I wonder where Daniel is hiding," Violet said as she watched the smoke rise from the obsidian house.

18
HOME AGAIN

Hannah looked out at the village, happy to see the townspeople strolling in and out of the shops that lined the busy streets. "It's funny. I don't even know which townspeople used to be rainbow griefers," she said with a smile.

"I'm so happy that the griefers were able to adjust to a world of freedom. But I really worry that Daniel is going to want serious revenge on us," Violet said. She could imagine daily attacks from the Ender Dragon and the Wither, and a neverending battle against hostile mobs that Daniel could spawn. And after he replenished his rainbow griefer army there would be more attacks.

Ben walked over with his dog Hope. "I thought there was going to be a feast to celebrate our victory?"

"Yes," answered Noah and he took cake from his inventory. "I have cake, what do you guys have for the feast?"

Hannah placed apples beside the obsidian house and then climbed to the top of the house and made an announcement: "Everybody, we are having a feast! Bring whatever goodies you have in your inventories and share it with us! We are here to celebrate our victory."

The townspeople gathered by the obsidian house, bringing all sorts of treats to share with each other. From potatoes to chicken, everyone feasted and celebrated their new freedom. Violet was the only one who didn't feel at ease. She worried about Daniel. She wasn't going to be happy until Daniel was stopped and could no longer attack the people in the Overworld.

The sun was setting and the townspeople cleared out from the center of town. Before nightfall, Violet took a walk through the streets of the village. She passed Valentino's butcher shop and the library. Violet loved her town and she wanted to protect the people from Daniel and his evil ways. As the sky grew darker, Violet heard Noah call out, "Violet, you should head back to the tree house! It's not safe in the streets."

Violet hurried to the tree house, she climbed the ladder, and said good night to Noah. They deserved a good night of sleep. Violet climbed into her bed and pulled the blue wool covers over her tired body. She knew that whatever happened next, at least she'd respawn in her own comfy bed.

THE END

DO YOU LIKE FICTION FOR MINECRAFTERS?

Check out other unofficial Minecrafter adventures from Sky Pony Press!

Invasion of the
Overworld
MARK CHEVERTON

Battle for the
Nether
MARK CHEVERTON

Confronting the
Dragon
MARK CHEVERTON

Trouble in
Zombie-town
MARK CHEVERTON

The Quest for the
Diamond Sword
WINTER MORGAN

The Mystery of
the Griefer's Mark
WINTER MORGAN

The Endermen
Invasion
WINTER MORGAN

Treasure Hunters
in Trouble
WINTER MORGAN

Available wherever books are sold!

LIKE OUR BOOKS FOR MINECRAFTERS?

Then check out other novels by Sky Pony Press.

Pack of Dorks
BETH VRABEL

Boys Camp: Zack's Story
CAMERON DOKEY, CRAIG ORBACK

Boys Camp: Nate's Story
KITSON JAZYNKA, CRAIG ORBACK

Letters from an Alien Schoolboy
R. L. ASQUITH

Just a Drop of Water
KERRY O'MALLEY CERRA

Future Flash
KITA HELMETAG MURDOCK

Sky Run
ALEX SHEARER

Mr. Big
CAROL AND MATT DEMBICKI

Available wherever books are sold!